# SMART KIDS ROCK

Written & Designed
by
A.S. Roper

Young boys and girls turn on their superpowers every day when they enter school.

Smart friends enjoy school.

Little Boys and Girls are known to have...

superpowers.

These powers make little girls and boys a...

school Rock Star.

This smart girl likes to read Mystery.

This smart boy likes to read History.

There is a smart boy who knows his ABC's.

This smart boy studies numbers too.

Smart girls like school...

Smart boys are cool.

There are superpowers in knowing how to count.

Friends will ask: "What is the total amount?"

Reading and Writing are fun things to do in class.

The teacher shows the facts.

Friends smile and chat as they enjoy school lunch.

Smart students practice good manners.

Smart boys and girls play nice during Art.

# The Library is where kids discover their smarts.

WE READ WE LEAD

Using school superpowers is not very hard...

but their superpowers must be recharged.

The trick to recharge the school superpowers,
is a smart kid's secret to keep.

The smartest kids know the secret is in a good night's sleep.

# The End

CPSIA information can be obtained
at www.ICGtesting.com
Printed in the USA
LVRC012147190720
661100LV00001B/11

9 780578 593142